Millicent Scowlworthy

by Rob Handel

A SAMUEL FRENCH ACTING EDITION

SAMUEL FRENCH

FOUNDED 1830

NEW YORK HOLLYWOOD LONDON TORONTO

SAMUELFRENCH.COM

Copyright © 2010 by Rob Handel

ALL RIGHTS RESERVED

CAUTION: Professionals and amateurs are hereby warned that *MILLI-CENT SCOWLWORTHY* is subject to a Licensing Fee. It is fully protected under the copyright laws of the United States of America, the British Commonwealth, including Canada, and all other countries of the Copyright Union. All rights, including professional, amateur, motion picture, recitation, lecturing, public reading, radio broadcasting, television and the rights of translation into foreign languages are strictly reserved. In its present form the play is dedicated to the reading public only.

The amateur and professional live stage performance rights to *MILLICENT SCOWLWORTHY* are controlled exclusively by Samuel French, Inc., and licensing arrangements and performance licenses must be secured well in advance of presentation. PLEASE NOTE that amateur Licensing Fees are set upon application in accordance with your producing circumstances. When applying for a licensing quotation and a performance license please give us the number of performances intended, dates of production, your seating capacity and admission fee. Licensing Fees are payable one week before the opening performance of the play to Samuel French, Inc., at 45 W. 25th Street, New York, NY 10010.

Licensing Fee of the required amount must be paid whether the play is presented for charity or gain and whether or not admission is charged.

Stock/professional licensing fees quoted upon application to Samuel French, Inc.

For all other rights than those stipulated above, apply to: The Gersh Agency, 41 Madison Avenue, New York, NY 10010; attn: Joseph Rosswog.

Particular emphasis is laid on the question of amateur or professional readings, permission and terms for which must be secured in writing from Samuel French, Inc.

Copying from this book in whole or in part is strictly forbidden by law, and the right of performance is not transferable.

Whenever the play is produced the following notice must appear on all programs, printing and advertising for the play: "Produced by special arrangement with Samuel French, Inc."

Due authorship credit must be given on all programs, printing and advertising for the play.

ISBN 978-0-573-69878-1   Printed in U.S.A.   #29683

No one shall commit or authorize any act or omission by which the copyright of, or the right to copyright, this play may be impaired.

No one shall make any changes in this play for the purpose of production.

Publication of this play does not imply availability for performance. Both amateurs and professionals considering a production are strongly advised in their own interests to apply to Samuel French, Inc., for written permission before starting rehearsals, advertising, or booking a theatre.

No part of this book may be reproduced, stored in a retrieval system, or transmitted in any form, by any means, now known or yet to be invented, including mechanical, electronic, photocopying, recording, videotaping, or otherwise, without the prior written permission of the publisher.

MUSIC USE NOTE

Licensees are solely responsible for obtaining formal written permission from copyright owners to use copyrighted music in the performance of this play and are strongly cautioned to do so. If no such permission is obtained by the licensee, then the licensee must use only original music that the licensee owns and controls. Licensees are solely responsible and liable for all music clearances and shall indemnify the copyright owners of the play and their licensing agent, Samuel French, Inc., against any costs, expenses, losses and liabilities arising from the use of music by licensees.

IMPORTANT BILLING AND CREDIT
REQUIREMENTS

All producers of *MILLICENT SCOWLWORTHY must* give credit to the Author of the Play in all programs distributed in connection with performances of the Play, and in all instances in which the title of the Play appears for the purposes of advertising, publicizing or otherwise exploiting the Play and/or a production. The name of the Author *must* appear on a separate line on which no other name appears, immediately following the title and *must* appear in size of type not less than fifty percent of the size of the title type.

In addition the following credit *must* be given in all programs and publicity information distributed in association with this piece:

Originally Presented Off-Broadway at The Summer Play Festival

MILLICENT SCOWLWORTHY was supported by a residency and public staged readings at the 2002 O'Neill Playwrights Conference of the Eugene O'Neill Theatre Center, Waterford, CT

MILLICENT SCOWLWORTHY was first presented at The Summer Play Festival on July 5, 2006. The performance was directed by Ken Rus Schmoll, with sets by Sue Rees, costumes by Meghan E. Healey, lighting by Garin Marschall, sound by Leah Gelpe, music direction and arrangements by Michael Pettry, musical assistance by Chris Speed, choreography by Gabriella Barnstone, and dramaturgy by Beatrice Basso. The production stage manager was Charles M. Turner III. The cast was as follows:

GIRL 1/KELLY . . . . Maria Dizzia

GIRL 2/MILLICENT . . . . Hannah Cabell

GIRL 3/REESE SCOWLWORTHY . . . . .Megan Hart

GIRL 4/IGGY SMICK . . . . Laura Tamayo

GIRL 5/SASS . . . . .Emily Sophia Knapp

BOY 1/PORTER SCOWLWORTHY . . . . Dan McCabe

BOY 2/HENRY . . . . .Debargo Sanyal

BOY 3/TIM THE CATER-WAITER . . . . .Joe Curnutte

BOY 4/HAMILTON SCOLWORTHY . . . . Greg Keller

BOY 5/JINX PORBEAGLE . . . . .Jonathan Monk

BOY 6/JAKE THE STRANGE KID . . . . John Summerour

BOY 7 (THE WAITER)/BOTHO SPIRE . . . . Alexis Camins

MILLICENT SCOWLWORTHY was developed at the 2002 O'Neill Playwrights Conference (James Houghton, artistic director). It was directed by Daniel Goldstein, with dramaturgy by Megan Monaghan. The cast included Noah Bean, Michael Chernus, Jesse Tyler Ferguson, Dara Fisher, Brent Popolizio, Susan Pourfar, Rhea Seehorn, Samantha Soule, and Matthew Stadelmann.

CHARACTERS

GIRL 1 / KELLY VANDERSLICE
GIRL 2 / MILLICENT
GIRL 3 / REESE SCOWLWORTHY
GIRL 4 / IGGY SMICK
GIRL 5 / SASS TENDRIL
BOY 1 / PORTER SCOWLWORTHY
BOY 2 / HENRY VANDERSLICE
BOY 3 / TIM THE CATER-WAITER
BOY 4 / HAMILTON SCOWLWORTHY
BOY 5 / JINX PORBEAGLE
BOY 6 / JAKE THE STRANGE KID
BOY 7 (THE WAITER) / BOTHO SPIRE

SETTING

Act One: An overgrown memorial
Act Two: An all-night diner
Act Three: A living room

ACT ONE

(A glade. A full moon. An overgrown memorial: several rows of miniature [smaller than life-sized], old-fashioned school desks. Maybe they're made of wood, or maybe they're made of a more otherworldly material like Lucite. Two benches downstage for those who wish to contemplate. A large open area at center.)

*(Enter **GIRL 1** with a school backpack. She drops it and goes directly to face the rows of desks. She kneels.)*

*(After a few moments, enter **GIRL 2**, also high school age. She stands regarding the desks. She removes her earphones.)*

GIRL 2. Where's the plaque?

GIRL 1. Maybe they're cleaning it or something.

GIRL 2. I know it by heart. In memory of the victims of the atrocity at Olympus Microsystems High School. The innocents will live forever in our hearts. Then the list of names.

GIRL 1. You know the names by heart?

GIRL 2. 'Course. You have to. I know the birthdays too.

*(Enter **BOY 1** with a large, ragged cardboard box. He puts it on the ground, center.)*

BOY 1. Did you see they took away the plaque?

GIRL 1. How long's it been gone?

BOY 1. A while.

GIRL 2. It was here last time.

GIRL 1. You think they'll take the desks?

BOY 1. I don't think they'd dare take the desks. But they'll stop mowing. They'll stop taking care of it.

GIRL 1. We'll mow.

BOY 1. Yes.

GIRL 2. We should say the names every time. We'll have to keep them. We'll have to pass them on.

BOY 1. Good idea.

(**GIRL 1** *shivers.*)

BOY 1. You OK?

GIRL 1. Cool tonight.

(**GIRL 1** *takes her backpack to one side and opens it.* **GIRL 2** *helps her unpack old, chipped, and clouded champagne glasses, bottles, and other barware.* **BOY 1** *moves about, arranging other props. More* **BOYS AND GIRLS** *arrive in ones and twos. The group of teenagers represents a cross section of high school demographics: goth, punk, geek, Prada, jock, stoner, etc. Everyone pauses for a moment in front of the desks upon entering. One crosses himself. Backpacks are piled at the edges of the stage. One of the boys has a guitar case.*)

GIRL 5. What happens right after the science lab?

GIRL 1. The mask.

GIRL 5. Oh yeah.

GIRL 2. I heard it used to be all written down. All of it.

GIRL 1. It was found in a composition book. It's lost now.

GIRL 2. Did they take it away?

GIRL 1. Maybe. Anyway it's safer not to write it down.

GIRL 2. Who found the composition book?

GIRL 1. I don't know. I was still in Montessori.

(*When the group is fully assembled – the whole cast except* **BOY 7**, *who is not in this act – two of the* **BOYS AND GIRLS** *begin to sing a song. It is a simple song in a strange language, a possibly misheard Slavic lullaby. All the* **BOYS AND GIRLS** *join in, singing quietly.*)

(*The* **BOYS AND GIRLS** *form a line that will take them past two stations manned by* **GIRL 5** *and* **BOY 6**. **BOY 6** *stands by the cardboard box.* **GIRL 5** *holds a fishbowl. In the fishbowl are nine ping pong balls. Each* **BOY/GIRL**, *without looking, fishes a ping pong ball out of the bowl; reads what is written on the ball; moves to* **BOY 6** *and gives him the ball.* **BOY 6** *reads the ball and hands the* **BOY/GIRL** *the corresponding item from the box.)*

(Each item is a simple costume element which the **BOY/ GIRL** *will add to their everyday clothes to take on a character: a brightly colored scarf, a hat, a tie, an oversize tuxedo jacket. There is brief amusement when two of the teenagers open their boxes to find they will be playing characters of the opposite sex:* **BOY 5** *gets a wig to play* **JINX**. **GIRL 4** *gets a fat-suit jacket and maybe a Tilley hat to play* **SMICK**.*)*

*(***GIRL 2** *is one of the last to pick. She is handed a spangle-covered, tasteless little dress and an enormous matching hair ribbon. She wanders downstage holding the dress in front of her, a relic and a burden.* **GIRL 3** *sees the dress and touches* **GIRL 2** *for a moment. A few others repeat this action.* **GIRL 2** *runs off into the woods with her costume.)*

(The song has ended. In silence, everyone puts on his or her costume piece.)

(The **BOYS AND GIRLS** *begin to hum "O Holy Night." The large cardboard box is moved to one side and turned upside down to serve as a table. A string of large Christmas bulbs is pulled from someone's backpack and wrapped around the nearest tree. The plug is left lying on the ground. Everyone sits on or around the two benches, facing center. "O Holy Night" ends.)*

*(***BOY 2** *takes out a cellphone and speaks into it, taking on the role of* **HENRY VANDERSLICE**. *During his speech, he takes a bottle and glass, moves to the "table" and mimes pouring.)*

HENRY. What do you mean you're stuck in Washington? Tomorrow is Christmas Eve, for crying out loud. It's Christmas Eve eve. The guests are drinking champagne but I just cracked a bottle of Wild Turkey that's only for you and me. No, I'm not going to tell you how old it is, get your ass on a plane and come look... Yeah, yeah, yeah. You big jerk. Look, if you can find the time, say Merry Christmas to Melanie for me. If she didn't find out yet, I gave a quarter mill to her breast cancer thing this year... Well, it's in Patricia's memory, you know... Nah, nah, nah. You have a hard-working merry time, all right?

(He puts away the phone as **TIM THE CATER-WAITER** *[***BOY 3***] enters the "stage" carrying an old truck tire with the help of another* **BOY/GIRL**. *Enter* **KELLY VANDERSLICE** *[***GIRL 1***] opposite, adjusting her clothes.)*

KELLY. Dad? Is this hooked in back?

(sees the tire)

That whole cake is for Millicent? Isn't she like nine years old?

HENRY. That's right. She'll be on a sugar high for days.

KELLY. I can't wait to see who pops out of it.

HENRY. I knew I forgot something. Has Prince William's car arrived?

(He smiles at **TIM** *as he says this.* **TIM** *smiles back, not sure if this is a joke.)*

KELLY. Prince William is a butthole.

HENRY. Kelly.

KELLY. He only wants to talk about his horse. He's a total boy. And he's stuck up.

HENRY. He *is* the heir to the throne.

KELLY. So? The Prince of Monaco isn't stuck up.

HENRY. Maybe that's because he's heir to the throne of *Monaco*. Anyway, I was joking. Prince William isn't coming tonight.

KELLY. You should have invited the Prince of Monaco.

HENRY. No princes are coming.

KELLY. Now *he* could pop out of my cake.

HENRY. NO ONE IS GOING TO POP OUT OF THE CAKE.

BOY 1. *(from the "audience")* Ring ring.

HENRY. *(answering cell phone)* Arlen! Happy Hanukah!

(HENRY exits. TIM has lined up glasses on the table; he mimes filling them from the bottle. KELLY takes one.)

KELLY. Why, thank you...

TIM. Tim.

KELLY. Thank you, Tim the cater-waiter.

TIM. I can get you a coke or something if you'd rather.

KELLY. Don't be afraid. I'm nineteen.

TIM. *(not fooled)* So you live here? ...When you're home from college?

KELLY. Did you get the tour? The ballroom is great for blading.

TIM. How many rooms do you have?

KELLY. Just my bedroom. It's got a safari theme. Why?

TIM. I meant how many rooms does the house have.

KELLY. I never counted.

(examining the "cake")

It's not like it's not big enough. For someone to jump out of. Or into.

(She has already drained her champagne and holds it out to TIM for a refill. He obliges. They watch each other. TIM indicates the cake.)

TIM. Who's Millicent?

KELLY. You know, the little orphan from Kosovo or whatever? Our next door neighbors adopted her. Mr. Scowlworthy, you know, Olympus Microsystems? They saw her on Rosie O'Donnell. Everyone wanted to adopt her after that show. There was like a bidding war. Her name used to be Millicent Hrynyszyn, now it's Millicent Scowlworthy.

TIM. Her name was what?

KELLY. Hrynyszyn.

(She giggles.)

TIM. You pronounce that very well.

KELLY. I speak Kos. Fluidly. I'm fluid in Kos.

TIM. Are you sure I'm not going to be in trouble when your dad comes back and finds you all giggly?

KELLY. You're right. Hide me.

*(Without warning, **KELLY** swoons into **TIM**'s arms. **HENRY** returns, still on his phone. **TIM** tries to stand **KELLY** up, but she remains obstinately limp.)*

HENRY. *(into phone)* Listen, people are starting to arrive. Give everyone my love.

*(He hangs up. To **TIM**, evenly.)*

Maybe there's something you can do in the kitchen.

TIM. Yes, sir.

*(He exits. **HENRY** relieves **KELLY** of her champagne glass.)*

HENRY. Joy to the world. Thank God I don't have one of those spoiled, badly behaved teenagers you always read about in the Rocky Mountain News. Someday you're going to get yourself into a situation you can't get out of by calling me.

KELLY. *(drunk)* Like last summer when you got me that internship with Marty Lewis? Marty Lewis who even though he had a billion dollar company to run managed to find the time to teach me how to use the computer, to ask me whether I was learning a lot, to tell me about his plane and his boat. Who one morning goes, "I think you're ready for the big leagues." I look at the computer and he's set up an account for a new trader named Mel Burr. I go, who's he? He goes, he's you. I start with a $150,000 portfolio. I watch the ticker scroll across the screen, I watch the numbers rise and fall, I keep an eye on the news. I punch in trades. All around me men are cursing and spilling coffee and screaming into the phone and banging on their computer monitors. I feel Marty Lewis's breath on my hair. I swivel around. He goes, "How did you do?" I go, "I think I did well, Mr. Lewis." "Did you like it?" He's looking at something on the desk. I follow his eyes. It's my hand, hovering over the mouse, quivering. I know what this is. This is money. This is sex. I go, "It was OK."

BOY 4. *(from the audience)* Ding dong.

*(*TIM *returns.)*

HENRY. I'll get it. Why don't you fetch a nice mug of hot cocoa for my daughter, and put some strong black coffee in it.

TIM. Yes, sir.

(Exit TIM *and* HENRY *in opposite directions. Enter from the direction of* HENRY's *exit* HAMILTON SCOWL-WORTHY [BOY 4], PORTER SCOWLWORTHY [BOY 1], REESE SCOWLWORTHY [GIRL 3], *and* MILLICENT [GIRL 2]. *They mime brushing snow from their coats.* MILLICENT *in her red and green dress and ribbon looks like a gift-wrapped doll.)*

REESE. Look at the tree! Look at the cake! It's for you! Can you read what it says?

PORTER. Hey.

KELLY. Hey.

HAMILTON. Kelly, this our new daughter Millicent.

KELLY. Hi.

HAMILTON. Kelly goes to the high school with Porter.

*(*MILLICENT *stares fixedly at* KELLY.)*

REESE. She's still shy about speaking English. Champagne!

*(*REESE *and* HAMILTON *take glasses from the table.* TIM *reappears with cocoa mugs for* KELLY *and* PORTER. *Throughout the following,* TIM *is occupied with ferrying glasses and bottles, ladling from punch bowls at the table, slicing limes with a paring knife, and so on.* HENRY *returns.)*

HENRY. Sorry, the doorbell keeps ringing. Everyone happy with a drink?

HAMILTON. Excellent.

PORTER. Is Professor Hawking coming up from Aspen?

HENRY. I think he's in England. Did you meet him here last winter?

PORTER. Yes, we found a lot to talk about.

REESE. They play chess on the Internet.

HENRY. Kelly, show Millicent the house.

KELLY. You want to see the house?

> (**MILLICENT** *stares at her.*)

HENRY. *(to* **HAMILTON***)* There's someone in the pool room I want you to meet.

> (**HENRY** *exits with* **HAMILTON** *and* **REESE.***)*

KELLY. *(to* **MILLICENT***)* You like computer games?

MILLICENT. They used duct tape made in the U.S. so we couldn't scream. Detroit, M.I.

> *(pause)*

KELLY. Does she always say things like that?

PORTER. That's the most words I've ever heard her speak.

KELLY. How long since she came?

PORTER. About two months.

KELLY. Must be a nightmare.

PORTER. My mom's happy. My mom's delighted. She always wanted a girl.

KELLY. In like a weird way?

PORTER. You mean like did she make me wear a dress?

KELLY. Did she?

PORTER. No.

KELLY. You had me worried.

PORTER. Why? Don't you think I'd look good in a dress?

KELLY. Depends on the dress.

PORTER. You could pick it out.

KELLY. Where do you shop?

PORTER. You tell me. I put myself in your hands.

KELLY. What's your budget?

PORTER. Let's say unlimited. It's for a special occasion.

KELLY. They won't let you try on a dress, Porter.

PORTER. I'll wear a wig. I'll have a brilliant disguise. Padded bra. Full drag. We'll go in the dressing room together.

KELLY. What's your bra size?

PORTER. I guess that's an open question. What would look proportional?

*(He poses for her. They both notice **MILLICENT**, who is still staring at **KELLY**.)*

KELLY. *(to **MILLICENT**)* Did you want to see the house?

MILLICENT. Bonfires of sisters. It was day all the time. They put us on sticks.

KELLY. Who did?

MILLICENT. When the blue helmets came, like men with the shells of bird's eggs, they gave us cake.

HAMILTON. *(to **HENRY**, as they return)* You're going to get me in trouble. You know Reese doesn't allow anyone to have a bigger tree than we do.

MILLICENT. *(so that only **KELLY** can hear)* There's still blood on the floor of my house where they left me.

KELLY. Stop talking like that.

*(Enter **JINX PORBEAGLE [BOY 5]**.)*

JINX. Are you Millicent? Oh you must be, with that festive dress. Aren't you an angel?

HAMILTON. Jinx, Merry Christmas.

(He kisses her cheek.)

JINX. It's the proud father. Are all these people too much for her?

HAMILTON. She's still shy about speaking English.

JINX. I bet Reese made that adorable dress.

HAMILTON. You know Reese. I tell her we don't need to sew our own clothes anymore but there's no stopping her.

HENRY. Hey, don't complain.

(During the following, **MILLICENT** *circles around the cake, studying but not touching it.* **KELLY** *and* **PORTER** *talk in a corner, drinking their cocoa.)*

JINX. That's right, this way you'll never have to cut up her credit card. Now before I have any champagne I need to talk to both of you.

HENRY. Uh-oh.

JINX. That's right, it's about the arts council. Is Joe coming tonight?

HENRY. The mayor? He had to christen a tree or something.

JINX. We had a very exciting meeting with him yesterday. I don't have to tell you about the strides this town has made in growing a bigger star on the cultural map. With the renovation of the performing arts center this year –

HAMILTON. *(joking to* **HENRY***)* That's right, how could she possibly want more money?

JINX. We have a project in mind for next fall that will solidify our position as a national culture destination. You will see hotels booked solid months in advance. You will see coverage in major papers around the world.

HAMILTON. That so?

JINX. An epic retelling of Greek myths. A theatrical event of record proportions, directed by Botho Spire.

HENRY. Who is?

JINX. A very hot director from Europe. Critics love him.

HAMILTON. You've got his commitment?

JINX. Once he approves the budget.

HENRY. Ah, the budget.

JINX. We have a massive promotional campaign set to go national with the airline partner, the hotel partners, the restaurant partners for dinner breaks – you can fly in and see the show over several nights or in a day-long marathon.

HAMILTON. How long is this damn play?

HENRY. Who's the cast?

JINX. Primarily local actors, members of the community. There are all kinds of tie-in workshops –

HENRY. What about Kelly?

JINX. *(momentarily thrown off her game)* Kelly…

HENRY. Can rehearsals be scheduled around school?

JINX. Of course, Kelly!

HENRY. There's got to be a part in all of Greek myth…

HAMILTON. I forgot to tell you, we saw her commercial the other night. With the bubble gum.

HENRY. You should have seen the pilot she did for Fox. Unfortunately, no one did.

JINX. Our homegrown actress.

HENRY. Come and see me Tuesday.

JINX. Thank you, Henry.

HAMILTON. If it's good for the city, Olympus wants to be a part of it, you know that's what I always say.

JINX. I'll drink to that. Where's that champagne?

*(Enter **REESE**.)*

REESE. Porter, your friend Cameron is here.

PORTER. *(as he exits past her)* He's not my friend, he's my familiar.

REESE. I only understand half of what he says. He's always on the computer playing some game about Attila the Hun. Or else he's in the quantum physics chatroom.

HAMILTON. At least that's what he says.

REESE. Well, whenever I look at the screen there's all kinds of Greek letters. So if he's chatting about something nasty, at least he's learning a classical language.

HENRY. I'm sure he's not doing anything abnormal for a boy his age.

HAMILTON. He knows I'd kill him if he did.

*(**HENRY** and **HAMILTON** chuckle.)*

JINX. Millicent looks adorable.

REESE. Doesn't she? I'm trying to figure out which outfit she should wear when she goes on Rosie with her new family.

JINX. Tell us when!

HENRY. Is she starting school here after the holiday?

REESE. We hope so. Right now we're just trying to get her comfortable with the language and the new environment. She's still a little shell-shocked, poor thing. I sense sometimes that she's having a flashback, you know. The first week, she'd wake up when the garbage men started banging around. I heard something coming from her room and I peeked through the door to see this lump under the blanket whimpering like a little puppy. It broke your heart. I said a quick prayer and sat on the edge of the bed, but I didn't know whether it would scare her if I touched the little lump, so I tried to make my voice very soothing, like the ocean. "Millicent? It's your mommy. It's all right. You're safe here. No one's going to shoot you. You're in the United States."

JINX. Did she come out from under the blanket?

REESE. No, it got to be time to get her dressed so I had to kind of fold back the sheets until she popped out.

HENRY. You're a very generous woman to take on this responsibility, Reese.

JINX. Everyone admires what you two have done.

HAMILTON. I just wish I could spend more time at home.

HENRY. *(to* **JINX***)* This guy loves kids. I remember when Porter was born – this was when he used to work for me – every day he'd come in, "You won't believe what Porter did today." "Aw, Porter spit up on my tie." Drove us all nuts. We'd go out for lunch and he'd be, "I'll be right back, I just want to buy something for Porter." There was a sporting goods store across the street from the office. He's bringing back a catcher's mitt, an umpire's mask, a little bat – enough equipment for a whole Little League team. Mind you, this was before Porter could walk.

HAMILTON. I figured he'd be ready by the time we got a major league team here.

HENRY. He was not happy to live in a state with no team.

HAMILTON. I decided I'd have to change that.

JINX. So that's why we have that stadium.

(All laugh.)

HAMILTON. Listen. When I was a kid, we didn't have much money. My dad worked all the time. We never saw him. I barely knew what he looked like. But one Sunday – it was the first real summer day – I hear a noise from the garage, and it's my dad rooting around for something. He pulls out a baseball with the leather barely hanging on it, and a couple of old gloves, and he says, "You want to toss a ball around?" I never forgot that day. He died when I was in college. I came back to visit him in the hospital. He couldn't talk, what with the oxygen mask and everything, but I came in and I said, "Hey Dad, you want to toss a ball around?" And he smiled.

(Pause. The others smile.)

Porter never did learn to catch. Or throw. But he is a master of the disparaging look.

KELLY. *(conspiratorily, to* **TIM***)* Is it your job to spike the eggnog?

TIM. You think I'm going to tell you?

KELLY. You want to go get high?

TIM. Where?

KELLY. Upstairs, third door on the right.

TIM. If I can sneak away.

KELLY. 'kay.

*(***TIM*** exits with a tray of empty glasses.)*

HENRY. Everyone else is eating. Kelly, keep Millicent entertained while I make sure her parents get some food.

KELLY. *(hissing)* No way. She weirds me utterly.

HENRY. Just watch her for a minute while we check out the buffet. Anything you recommend?

KELLY. I don't eat.

HENRY. Oh, that's right.

JINX. *(of* **MILLICENT,** *as they go out)* She can't take her eyes off that cake. Who can blame her?

(Exit **HENRY, HAMILTON, REESE,** *and* **JINX. KELLY** *watches nervously as* **MILLICENT** *explores the Christmas tree.* **MILLICENT** *glances up at* **KELLY,** *who takes an involuntary half-step backward.* **MILLICENT** *returns to her investigation, then suddenly disappears behind the tree. All is still. Tentatively,* **KELLY** *approaches the tree. She peeks behind it. She looks in front of it again. She looks behind it again, and disappears behind it.* **MILLICENT** *emerges from under the tree. She starts to tug at a string of tree lights.* **KELLY** *emerges from behind the tree, sees* **MILLICENT** *loosening the string of lights, and goes to take the lights away from her.* **MILLICENT** *stops her with a look.* **KELLY** *tries to move in gently;* **MILLICENT** *flinches, causing* **KELLY** *to balk. Satisfied that* **KELLY** *has given up,* **MILLICENT** *returns to pulling the string off the tree.* **KELLY** *looks around for help.* **KELLY** *decides to take no responsibility, and walks away.* **MILLICENT** *turns upstage and plays with the string of lights.* **KELLY** *hears a strange crunching sound. She rushes to* **MILLICENT** *and spins her around by the shoulders.* **MILLICENT** *is chewing the bulbs, one by one, the string disappearing into her mouth.* **KELLY** *covers her own mouth and staggers backward.* **MILLICENT** *talks with her mouth full.)*

MILLICENT. Once I bit off a man. He wanted to kill me except there was an American with a camera.

*(***KELLY** *dives behind the tree and mimes pulling the plug.* **KELLY** *runs to the table, grabs the paring knife, returns to* **MILLICENT,** *looks around quickly, and cuts the string of lights to the left and right of* **MILLICENT***'s head.* **KELLY** *picks* **MILLICENT** *up and carries her offstage.)*

(Enter **PORTER** *from the opposite side. He looks at the tree inquisitively. Enter* **IGGY SMICK [GIRL 4].***)*

SMICK. Nog!

(He oozes over to the table and takes a swig from a glass.)

This is my favorite time of year. Some people hate nog. To me that's like hating life. Can I get you one?

PORTER. I'm lactose intolerant.

SMICK. You must be Johnny Intolerant's son. Nice to meet you. I'm kidding.

PORTER. I got it.

SMICK. Iggy Smick. I'm doing some work for Mr. Vanderslice.

PORTER. Porter Scowlworthy.

SMICK. I like your glasses. Very distinguished. Aren't those the ones Elton John models?

PORTER. I believe so.

SMICK. How much did you pay for those?

PORTER. I couldn't tell you.

SMICK. I can get you those glasses for 29 bucks. No lie.

PORTER. How about these pants?

SMICK. The pants?

PORTER. How much for these pants?

SMICK. I don't think I have a pants connection, but I'll check my Rolodex. You don't know what a Rolodex is. I'll check my PalmPilot.

PORTER. Do you play chess?

SMICK. Poker's more my game.

PORTER. I would have picked you for a chess player.

SMICK. I can never remember how the pieces move.

PORTER. Too bad. That's the most important thing.

SMICK. *(taking a second eggnog)* Those bishops make me nervous. I was raised by nuns.

(**HENRY, HAMILTON, REESE** *and* **JINX** *return with plates.*)

HENRY. Hey, glad you could make it. This is my new overseas research consultant, Iggy Smick. Hamilton Scowlworthy, his wife Reese, Jinx Porbeagle.

REESE. Nice to meet you.

(**HENRY** *leaves the group and exits.*)

SMICK. I think we met once when I was with Pan-Euro's Special Situations Fund. Don't you have a place in Concocoot?

HAMILTON. Just a little ski cabin.

SMICK. I grew up there.

HAMILTON. You're kidding.

SMICK. Yeah, I try to get back now and then.

REESE. We're going out there right after the new year.

SMICK. I'm supposed to visit my cousin. Maybe we can meet for cocoa.

HAMILTON. I didn't know anyone grew up in Concocoot.

SMICK. We're a strange mountain tribe. I'll teach you the handshake – you'll notice you don't get charged as much at the deli.

(*to* **JINX**)

Wasn't Henry telling me about you and the library...?

JINX. The arts council?

SMICK. Of course. You know, I used to book tours for folk dance groups. Romanian, Belgian. Polka. I have some names if you're interested.

(*The adults drift upstage. Enter* **KELLY**, *urgently, to* **PORTER**.)

KELLY. (*whispering*) Have you seen Millicent?

PORTER. No.

KELLY. She got away. Help me find her.

(**SMICK** *approaches suddenly, startling* **KELLY**.)

SMICK. A crisis! A lovely young lady is blocking the eggnog!

PORTER. Kelly Vanderslice, this is Iggy Smick, an expert in eyewear.

(**PORTER** *slips out.*)

KELLY. Nice to meet you. Have you seen a little girl with a bizarre Christmas dress?

SMICK. No, have you lost one?

KELLY. Yeah.

SMICK. Well, let's go find her. If you were her, where would you be?

KELLY. Dead, I think.

SMICK. Come again?

KELLY. Or hiding.

SMICK. Why don't you go that way, and I'll go this way.

(*Enter* **HENRY**, *leading an unwilling* **MILLICENT** *by the hand.* **MILLICENT** *has been cleaned up.*)

KELLY. There she is!

HENRY. She was wandering around in the kitchen. Where has that cater-waiter gone?

KELLY. I was cleaning her up in the bathroom and she disappeared.

SMICK. So you're the little fugitive.

(**SMICK** *pats* **MILLICENT**'s *head. She does not flinch. The other adults come forward.*)

REESE. Millicent, are you enjoying the party?

(**MILLICENT** *places a hand on* **SMICK**'s *cheek, looking into his eyes.*)

MILLICENT. You don't have to be afraid. It will hurt a lot, but only for a second. You will leave a thing they can kick and rob and burn but it's not you. Where you will be there are sweet, sweet frogs with broad, warm tongues. You will be happy there. You will smile a real smile. It's all right, Ignatz. You are so close.

(**MILLICENT** *walks away from* **SMICK** *and sits on the floor to tie her shoe. Everyone is silent.* **SMICK** *is paralyzed for a moment. He becomes aware of the silence and tries to think of something funny to say, but draws a blank.*)

(The moment is broken by furious shouting offstage.
TIM *comes hurtling onstage backward, followed by*
PORTER, *who tackles him. They wrestle on the floor,* **TIM**
quickly gaining the advantage and ending up on top.
HAMILTON*'s voice booms through the general uproar.)*

HAMILTON. Let my son go right now.

*(***TIM** *releases* **PORTER** *and they separate warily, half col-*
lapsing. **HAMILTON** *strides up to* **TIM.***)*

HAMILTON. What's your name?

PORTER. I found him lurking in Kelly's bedroom.

TIM. I wasn't exactly lurking.

*(***PORTER** *launches himself at* **TIM** *again, but* **HAMIL-**
TON *blocks him.)*

HAMILTON. Take it easy.

*(***PORTER** *steps back, looks around for his glasses which*
have been knocked off in the fight, and takes his time
putting them back on and adjusting them.)

PORTER. *(to his father)* I wouldn't touch me if I were you.

(A strange pause. **HAMILTON** *turns back to* **TIM.***)*

HAMILTON. I think you'd better leave.

*(***TIM** *exits to the kitchen without a word.)*

REESE. Perhaps we'd better go too.

HENRY. Don't be silly, we haven't cut the cake yet.

REESE. I'm sorry. Millicent's tired. I need to get her to bed.

(Suddenly **MILLICENT** *is possessed by mortal terror.)*

MILLICENT. No.

HAMILTON. Millicent, behave.

HENRY. Well, if you think.

REESE. We'll just say our goodbyes.

MILLICENT. No, no, no!

(The **SCOWLWORTHYS** *are gathered in the middle of the*
room. Around them, **HENRY, JINX, KELLY,** *and the still*
shaken **SMICK.***)*

JINX. Sorry you can't stay.

REESE. *(to MILLICENT)* Say goodbye to your new friends.

MILLICENT. *(to KELLY)* I know you can't stop them from taking me.

HAMILTON. Don't worry about her. She had a terrible time over there.

(HAMILTON and REESE gently but forcefully move MILLICENT towards the exit as she continues to prophesy desperately at KELLY.)

MILLICENT. Wherever my body is dragged it leaves blood. Remember to always say what is happening. Don't pretend. Pretending only makes it worse. Don't be afraid. It's going to be just terrible.

(Exit the SCOWLWORTHYS. It's very quiet.)

HENRY. Excuse me while I speak to the caterers.

(He exits to the kitchen. KELLY goes to SMICK.)

KELLY. Have you got any matches?

(SMICK digs out a lighter and hands it to her.)

SMICK. Keep it. Something tells me it's time to give up smoking.

(He emits an awful little laugh.)

JINX. Oh listen, the others are singing carols.

(She disappears down the hall with an elaborate show of enthusiasm. HENRY returns.)

KELLY. *(hiding the lighter in her hand)* I think I'm going to go to bed now.

HENRY. *(as if nothing had happened)* Did Jinx tell you about the acting job?

KELLY. What acting job? An acting job for me?

HENRY. You should talk to her before she leaves.

(KELLY rushes off after JINX. HENRY and SMICK remain.)

HENRY. How about a last eggnog? Better yet, I've got this bottle of Wild Turkey. You want some?

SMICK. *(gamely attempting to seem himself)* Gobble, gobble.

(**HENRY** *pours drinks.*)

HENRY. What was Christmas like in Montana?

SMICK. Oh, gorgeous.

HENRY. How long did you say you were there?

SMICK. Five years.

HENRY. What the heck were you doing?

SMICK. This guy was running his business from up there. Real eccentric guy, but brilliant. Autographed pictures of tennis stars. Vacations with them. Fantasy camps. Turns out they're crazy for that stuff in Hong Kong. Kuwait. Nepal. Low volume, huge profits. All you need is a FedEx guy and some phone lines. The guy liked isolation. You should see his ranch. You got a place like that, who needs people? I used to finish work by lunch and spend the rest of the day in the sauna lagoon.

(**KELLY** *rushes back in, excited, and rushes out again the other way.*)

You know what else they have in that county is the uranium mines. These old abandoned mines. They're radioactive. You just drive by them and your car will set off a Geiger counter for days. Big business in pilgrims.

HENRY. Pilgrims?

SMICK. People believe the mines cure things. Arthritis. They come from all over to sit in the mines for a few hours each day. People buy the land and set up hotels, put up billboards. Fill the mines with plastic Jesuses and stuff. I thought about buying some up myself. Health mines, they call them.

HENRY. Can't be good for you to live by one of those.

SMICK. I don't know, the people who ran them always seemed to have kind of a glow. No lie. Kind of like that girl.

HENRY. Who? Millicent?

SMICK. Maybe she lived by a mine in Kosovo.

HENRY. Maybe so.

(slight pause)

Did you hear that?

SMICK. What? – Like glass breaking?

HENRY. Something.

(slight pause)

Damn caterers.

*(**KELLY** returns, hyper.)*

KELLY. Dad? Can I show you my song? Oh, hi. Dad, I have to audition for that Greek show. Can I show you my song?

HENRY. They need you to do a song?

KELLY. You always have to have your song ready just in case.

HENRY. She took an audition workshop in L.A.

KELLY. *(to SMICK)* Don't laugh, OK?

*(**KELLY** sings "It's Only a Paper Moon," executing a carefully choreographed routine of Broadway moves. **HENRY** and **SMICK** watch, sliding into a stupor.)*

*(As the second verse begins, the other **BOYS AND GIRLS**, who are sitting on the benches as the "audience," hum a harmony part.)*

*(On the bridge of the song, all the **BOYS AND GIRLS** sing as the scene breaks and everyone moves across the stage, striking the Christmas lights and table, leaving the clearing empty for the next scene.)*

*(As the song ends, everyone is seated in the audience except for **KELLY** and **PORTER**, who sit on the ground, hands wrapped around their knees. There is a stifling silence. They have been sitting there for a long time.)*

KELLY. *(cont.)* Were you asleep?

PORTER. I never sleep.

KELLY. Were you on the computer?

PORTER. In the anime chatroom. The Japanese one. It was daytime in Japan.

KELLY. You have a Japanese keyboard?

PORTER. They like to use English. Japanese kids. I'm like a celebrity there.

(*pause*)

KELLY. (*of the next room*) What are they talking about in there?

PORTER. Going over it again.

KELLY. Who was here when they found her?

PORTER. Your dad. The two cops. The cops were upstairs. Your dad and my dad were looking in the basement. My dad had looked down there once but he didn't see her the first time. She was in the back room.

(*pause*)

My dad says we're going to the place in Hilton Head.

KELLY. When?

PORTER. Tomorrow. Tonight.

KELLY. Isn't there going to be a funeral?

PORTER. I guess we'll come back. He wants to get mom away. From the house.

KELLY. Oh. Uh-huh.

(*pause*)

I woke up at six o'clock and my dad wasn't there. Then the phone rang and he told me he was over here. Isn't it weird that I woke up right before he called?

(*pause*)

Just when he would have been in the basement with your dad, finding...?

(*pause*)

How are you doing?

PORTER. (*absent*) Huh?

KELLY. How are you doing?

PORTER. OK.

KELLY. Was she wrapped in the blanket like that?

PORTER. No. My dad wrapped her. And put her under the tree.

(pause)

KELLY. What did you do?

PORTER. My mom made us pray.

(pause)

KELLY. I was surprised when you beat up that guy. At the party.

PORTER. I can beat people up.

KELLY. I was just surprised.

PORTER. I'm stronger than I look.

(pause)

KELLY. I'm kind of tired.

PORTER. Go home. Go to sleep.

KELLY. I feel like I should do something.

PORTER. *(looks at her)* Do you?

*(Pause. **KELLY** opens her mouth to speak but stops at the sound of a distant siren. She and **PORTER** listen. The siren grows louder, approaching. All the **BOYS AND GIRLS** burst into action, gathering their backpacks and scattering. A police loudspeaker is heard, drawing ever nearer.)*

LOUDSPEAKER. This is an illegal gathering. Return to your homes. This is an illegal gathering.

*(**BOY 1** is among the last to leave the stage. He hisses to others departing the opposite way.)*

BOY 1. Fifteen minutes! The diner!

(The clearing is empty. The siren, now very loud, winds down.)

ACT TWO

(An all-night diner. This set is smaller than the set for Act One – maybe this set fits inside it.)

(Diner booths. A tall glass cabinet with rotating shelves of cakes and pies, and a long cabinet with more cakes. Visible through the windows, a full moon.)

(The restaurant is deserted except for **THE WAITER** *[a.k.a.* **BOY 7**], *high school age. He is sitting in the corner of a booth, half asleep, with his elbow on the table.)*

(Enter **BOY 2**, *with backpack. He slides into a booth.* **THE WAITER** *stands and exits.* **GIRL 1** *and* **GIRL 5** *enter and take another booth.* **THE WAITER** *returns with water and a menu for* **BOY 2**, *notices the two* **GIRLS** *and gives a small sigh. He serves* **BOY 2** *and exits again.)*

(The remaining **BOYS AND GIRLS** *filter in and occupy booths. None of them wear the costumes they took out of the box in Act One, except for* **BOY 1**, *who still wears* **PORTER**'s *glasses.)*

*(***THE WAITER** *circulates, distributing water and menus.)*

*(***GIRL 4** *is the last to appear. She spots* **BOY 2** *and sits opposite him. Though they are no longer wearing their costumes, they still inhabit the roles of* **HENRY** *and* **SMICK**.)*

HENRY. Good trip?

SMICK. I'll tell you, I had to have a hamburger as soon as I got back. At the airport.

HENRY. What did the king say?

SMICK. He's not used to the whole "king" thing yet. He still wants people to call him Mike. He says he's not satisfied with the test data on the T-616. He wants to conduct his own trials.

HENRY. *(sarcastic)* Sure, we'll let him try out the T-616 on a rent to buy basis. Let him blow up some of those guerilla fighters that are bothering him.

SMICK. I asked him who he thought he was dealing with.

HENRY. Just smile and say no. Then compliment the wine. You're doing a fine job.

SMICK. Thanks. What'd I miss?

HENRY. Things are the same.

GIRL 3. *(at another booth)* Buzz buzz.

HENRY. Send him in.

> *(to* **SMICK***)*

> Keep up the good work.

SMICK. Oh, you bet.

> *(***SMICK** *moves to an empty booth.* **BOY 4** [**HAMILTON**] *joins* **HENRY***.)*

HENRY. Hamilton. Isn't it time for us to play racquetball?

HAMILTON. As if you're not chicken.

HENRY. Who's chicken?

HAMILTON. Listen, you know I was going to throw a dinner for the play opening. For Kelly. I know this is a big thing for her.

HENRY. It's all she talks about. They have their first rehearsal tonight.

HAMILTON. Well, look, I don't know if we can be there. We're thinking of moving to Hilton Head full-time.

HENRY. I understand.

HAMILTON. But I want to throw her that dinner. I was talking to the mayor about hosting it in his name.

HENRY. You don't have to do that. Send her some flowers.

HAMILTON. I want to. It breaks my heart, Henry, after I put my life and soul into this town. To be looked at. At meetings. I can't go to the gym. Can't go out to dinner. People stare. Reese stares back. They look away. They whisper. They sneak a peek at us again. Reese goes over to their table. Asks them how they are – she knows everyone – asks them about their kids. They don't say much. Like we're trying to get information out of them so we can plot the perfect time to break in through their basement window and kill their kids.

HENRY. Let me get you a drink.

HAMILTON. You've been great. You and Kelly are practically the only ones who'll talk to us. Outside of the lawyers and TV people. If those morons could catch the guy it would all end. But they're not even looking for the guy. You know? They're not looking for the guy.

HENRY. It must be hard on Reese.

HAMILTON. Now this Peter Twitchell is running for D.A. on the promise that he'll arrest us. That's his platform. That's his commercial.

HENRY. To hell with all of them. Your job is to keep your family together. Don't let them tear you apart.

HAMILTON. I don't know what I'm going to do. Stay? Run? I don't know what's the right thing to do. I built this town up from nothing, you know why? Because I thought it was a safe place to raise children.

HENRY. You've got every bit of goddamn respect I have for staying this long. You don't have to prove anything to anyone.

HAMILTON. He's manic-depressive, I understand.

HENRY. Who? Peter Twitchell?

HAMILTON. Manic-depressive. Apparently it's common knowledge.

(**THE WAITER** *serves pie to* **GIRL 1 [KELLY]** *and* **GIRL 5**. **GIRL 5** *takes on the role of* **SASS TENDRIL**.)

SASS. My mom wanted me to ask if I could get a ride to rehearsal with you and your dad, and she'll pick me up after.

KELLY. Jesus. Look, Sass, I am really stressed out today.

SASS. Just say it's OK, otherwise I'll have to call my mom and get her out of a meeting and she'll be pissed. Is it that big a deal? We're probably going to get out early because of the special assembly.

KELLY. All we do is have special assemblies. They're not even special anymore.

SASS. You didn't hear about Jake?

KELLY. Jake, the strange kid?

SASS. He had to write a story for English and he got called on to read it because the teacher figured he hadn't done the assignment. But he'd written like this whole novel all about Millicent.

KELLY. Great.

SASS. He's going to get expelled.

KELLY. For writing a novel?

SASS. It was like a fairy tale about these people living in a house on top of a mountain. There's a little girl and her older brother and they have a big secret. One night the parents are out shining the mountain and the little girl goes to the brother and goes like, I can't go on holding the big secret inside, I'm going to tell. And he's like, you better not, and they're fighting, and he like grabs her and is going, you better not, you better not, and she like stops moving, and he lets go but she's dead.

KELLY. Will you shut up? I don't want to hear about Jake's sick crap.

(**BOY 6**, *taking on the role of* **JAKE THE STRANGE KID**, *brings over a piece of pie he has been served and joins them at their booth.*)

JAKE. But you haven't heard the best part.

(*The two girls look up at him.*)

The parents come home and they decide to protect the brother by making it look like a lion came into the house and chewed up the little girl.

SASS. I thought you'd be in the principal's office.

JAKE. They can't keep me there forever.

KELLY. How does the story end?

JAKE. Justice is done. It's like a story from the Bible.

KELLY. In the Bible the person killed by the lion turned out to not really be dead.

JAKE. In this case I'm pretty sure she's dead.

BOY 4. *(from another booth)* Ring ring.

    *(**JAKE** answers his cell.)*

JAKE. What?… Huh?… Yeah, tell him yes. I'll be home as soon as I can get out of here… No, tell him I won't talk to anyone else. OK.

    (puts away phone, smiles, leans back)

    Fox News Channel wants to talk to me.

KELLY. They must be really bored.

SASS. I talked to them last Christmas.

KELLY. Everyone talked to them last Christmas. Everyone talked to everyone last Christmas.

JAKE. I dare this school to expel me after I read my story on Fox.

    *(**BOY 1 [PORTER]** approaches the booth and stands holding a piece of pie.)*

PORTER. Hey Jake.

JAKE. Hey Porter.

PORTER. I hear you've gone into creative writing.

JAKE. Yeah, right.

PORTER. What are you working on?

JAKE. Getting out of here.

    *(**JAKE** and **SASS** take their pie and go.)*

KELLY. He's going to get his ass kicked one of these days.

PORTER. He's going to get his ass kicked at three-fifteen.

KELLY. Don't. Everyone knows Jake is crazy. He just loves attention. That's the only reason he listens to that sick music. If you beat him up, you'll just make him think he's getting to you.

    *(She sees that **PORTER** is not persuaded.)*

KELLY. *(cont.)* His story is already on TV. Somebody must have called their favorite reporter right after English. If you beat him up that'll be on TV too.

PORTER. I'm not going to beat him up. I'm going to kill him. I thought I'd make it look like a lion did it.

(pause)

Anyway, we're on TV every night. It won't make any difference.

KELLY. I can't believe you still go to school here. I mean, I really admire that.

PORTER. It's not very crowded, the Porter Scowlworthy fan club.

KELLY. I don't care.

(pause)

PORTER. Time for assembly. Time to talk about healing. We're all trying to heal.

(He barks like a dog.)

Heel, boy. Heel.

*(Barks some more. **PORTER** and **KELLY** slide out of the booth and go in different directions with their pie. At this point, **THE WAITER**, who has served pie to just about everyone in the room, makes a small change in his waiter uniform to indicate that he is taking on the role of **BOTHO SPIRE**. He hoists himself up to sit on the long cabinet of cakes, legs dangling.)*

SPIRE. Welcome to the first rehearsal. I'd like to thank each of you for your courage in joining me for this extraordinary project.

*(The **BOYS AND GIRLS** realize the **WAITER** is one of them. Taking over the diner, they clear the two large tables from center, so that by the end of his speech **SPIRE** has jumped up and is using the empty space surrounded by the booths as his stage, with clean, extravagant gestures.)*

SPIRE. *(cont.)* We believe that theatre began as the religious observances of the ancient Greeks. Only priests were permitted to stand on the stage and retell history – stories of heroism and death which everyone present knew by heart. Over many, many years – because ancient Greece was a magnificent civilization which took a long time to slide into decadence – two things changed. One day a priest, whom tradition calls Thespis, stepped forward from the chorus and spoke a solo, saying "I am Zeus." It wasn't that he had gone mad; he simply thought it was a better way to tell a story. The other development was the rise of playwrights, who competed against one another, all telling the same stories. As a result, the stories became morally complex. In fact, moral complexity reaches a peak with the Greek dramatists which it has yet to reattain. These are not psychological dramas. When we put on the mask, we erase psychology. We inhabit the icon of Helen. The icon of Achilles. We give up the tricks and crutches of our trade as actors, the ability to play the audience with a look, to ply the audience with emotion, to seduce the audience with sex. We stand back, with them, from the character, and show them Helen, show them Achilles. I, like you, am a mere human; here is Achilles. During the next eight weeks, we will create, here on this stage, a world of giants.

*(**HAMILTON** and **REESE** slide into a booth facing **SMICK**.)*

SMICK. Welcome to my office. There's a guy sells great roasted peanuts over by the tiger cage.

HAMILTON. I hope the offer is still open, Mr. Smick. I know we took a long time to think it over.

SMICK. I completely understand.

HAMILTON. We've become so terribly suspicious. Everything we've said has been twisted.

REESE. Millicent is a saint. People need to hear the life of Millicent. Not the death of Millicent. You met her. She was not like every other little girl.

SMICK. That's true.

REESE. She suffered so much in her short time with us. I mean us on earth. Caught in that terrible war. Her parents dead. Her sister dead. A symbol of the orphans of this world. Suffer the little child: that's what we want to call our book.

SMICK. Let me make a note.

REESE. Then to be taken from us with suddenness. With violence. Here in the country that gave her shelter. In the inn that did not turn her away. Snatched from the arms of her new mother. From her new family. The first family perhaps ever to love her.

HAMILTON. What we want to communicate is the horror we feel at the behavior of the police. People need to see this through our eyes. To know what it's like to look at your neighbors' children playing, and know that the police are not looking for the child-killer on the loose. Why are they not looking? Because they think you killed your own child.

REESE. Why so much suffering in one so young? Why? Because God asks the most of those he loves most deeply. Do you know what I think, Mr. Smick? I think Millicent knew. I think she knew and there were times she resisted. Times she wanted to say, take away this cup for I do not want to drink it. But she knew she could not refuse her fate. For it was a gift. It was love. It was a message to a cruel, violent world gone mad that we should all hear and know and listen to the story of Millicent. I am not ashamed. I am proud.

(beat)

SMICK. As I said, I have a friend who has a friend at Time Books. He told me to tell you: none of us want to see this turn into some kind of bidding war. I am writing a number on this piece of paper.

(He slides the paper over to them. They study it.)

*(**KELLY** stands behind the cake cabinet. **THE WAITER** has left a tray of water glasses on the cabinet, and now*

KELLY *pours water from one glass to another, conducting a scientific experiment, taking notes.* PORTER *appears somewhere behind her.)*

PORTER. Trying to blow up the school?

KELLY. You scared me.

PORTER. *(as a spot reporter, holding imaginary earphone to head)* Well, Connie, she was kind of a loner. Always hanging out in the science lab after school. The rumor was she made LSD and sold it to the other kids.

KELLY. I wish.

PORTER. Really? Yearning to open the doors of perception?

KELLY. I think the doors are already open.

PORTER. In this place? They would need to be blasted off their hinges.

KELLY. Could you stop talking about explosions? I'm mixing chemicals here.

PORTER. *(picking up her notes)* Determining the pH value of vinegar. Shouldn't you be wearing an asbestos suit?

KELLY. *(trying to get the notes back)* You want to help me do this so I can go home?

PORTER. Don't you have rehearsal tonight?

KELLY. No, that's why I'm making up for half a semester of chemistry homework.

(They are engaged in a tug of war over the notes.)

PORTER. What's it like playing those Greek heroines?

KELLY. It's a lot of memorizing.

PORTER. What are your parts again?

KELLY. Iphigeneia and Elektra.

PORTER. *(pulling harder)* Do you feel like a plaything of the gods? Do you feel a sense of destiny?

KELLY. *(a threat)* I feel a sense of your destiny.

(KELLY gives a tremendous yank and pulls the notes to her chest and PORTER with them. They are very close. Beat.)

(cont.) Do you remember that movie they used to show us when the science teacher was too bored to teach? It started with a boy sitting in a boat on the river and then it zoomed in to his arm, and the mosquito on his arm, and the mosquito's stinger, and the blood cells, and smaller and smaller until the atom? Then it zoomed out again to the boy in the boat and kept zooming out to the city, and the globe, and the planet, and the solar system, and the galaxy, and the universe? I used to do that. I would be sitting at lunch watching kids get their milk or their chocolate milk, and I would zoom out so they were just dots inside the school, and somewhere over the mountains were the cows the milk came from, and chocolate cows the chocolate milk came from, and I'd zoom out more so somewhere in Taiwan a girl was making the shirts the kids were wearing, and everywhere there were other kids in other schools, all getting their milk, all wearing shirts. It made me happy to be part of this picture – like Here was a big place. Then sometime when I was fourteen or fifteen I forgot how to do it. I couldn't zoom out anymore. Here started to get smaller. Now Here is very small – just big enough to hold me – so close around me it makes me want to scream.

PORTER. Maybe you're lonely in there.

KELLY. Maybe.

*(Beat. **PORTER**, suddenly shy, begins to move away. **KELLY** puts her arms around him and kisses him. The **BOYS AND GIRLS** make the sound of a strange, low wind blowing through the room. **GIRL 2** stands center and speaks with the voice of **MILLICENT**.)*

MILLICENT. It's very cold here.

KELLY. Oh my God –

MILLICENT. It's colder than I thought. The windows are covered with frost. You can't see unless you breathe on them hard.

PORTER. Millicent –

KELLY. Don't talk to her. Maybe she'll go away.

MILLICENT. *(covering her ears)* Don't pretend. Pretending only makes it worse.

KELLY. …Always say what is happening.

MILLICENT. *(uncovering her ears)* I knew you would see me.

KELLY. Are you OK? I'm sorry, that's stupid. I don't know what to ask.

MILLICENT. I lived under a wooden bridge for a whole winter and it wasn't this cold. I'm very angry.

PORTER. What should I do?

MILLICENT. Is someone talking?

KELLY. It's your brother.

MILLICENT. Tell him to shut up. I'm very mad at him.

PORTER. I can see you too.

KELLY. Shut up, Porter.

*(to **MILLICENT**)*

Why? What did he do?

MILLICENT. *(pointedly)* Nothing.

KELLY. We want to help you. What should we do?

MILLICENT. Make it end. There must be an end. I know it ends badly.

(about to go, turns back)

Stay close for warmth.

*(**GIRL 2 [MILLICENT]** leaves center and goes and sits down. **PORTER** and **KELLY** stare at the empty space where she stood. Long pause.)*

KELLY. Porter –

PORTER. Wait.

KELLY. – I have to ask you something.

PORTER. Shh. Get under the desk.

KELLY. What?

PORTER. Someone's coming. Hide.

(**KELLY** *hides behind the cabinet.* **PORTER** *pretends to be taking notes.* **JAKE** *slithers over, watching* **PORTER**.)

PORTER. *(not looking up)* Hello, Jake.

JAKE. Trying to blow up the school?

PORTER. No, if I was trying to blow up the school I'd get a truckload of ammonium nitrate, combine it with six to eight percent diesel oil, drill holes for the detonator wires and set a timer on a military blasting cap with RDX as a kicker.

JAKE. Where would you get a blasting cap?

PORTER. I'd probably ask you.

(**JAKE** *puts a cigarette in his mouth without lighting it.*)

JAKE. I might know a guy who knows a guy.

PORTER. Someone you met in your writing group? Part of your new literary circle?

JAKE. That one story just kinda came to me.

PORTER. I would have expected something more imaginative.

JAKE. Oh yeah?

PORTER. There are three basic theories, right? One: it was an accident. To protect someone in the family, the family decides to lie. Lies lead to more lies, and here we are. Two: it was a sexual abuse situation, she was going to tell, so the abuser, or abusers, kill her. The family decides to lie, et cetera. Three: it was a *very thin* intruder who came in the basement window after cleverly breaking it so that the glass ended up on the outside. – Not a very popular theory.

JAKE. I thought that was your favorite.

PORTER. Anyone who buys that theory looks like an idiot. On the other hand, if I don't buy that theory, my choices are that I'm a sex murderer, an accidental murderer, or an accomplice to one of the above. Some people might think being an idiot looks more attractive.

JAKE. Either way, you know who did it.

PORTER. You know what's funny? Everyone in school calls you Jake the Strange Kid. But whenever the tabloids write about me they call me Millicent's strange brother. The Scowlworthys' strange son.

JAKE. What's wrong with being strange?

PORTER. I guess it seems to me that what's strange is for a nine year-old girl to get the shit beaten out of her and die of blunt trauma to the head and then have a cord tied around her dead neck and twisted tighter and tighter gouging into her skin and for no one to be blamed. Like it just happened. It's too bad, but it just happened. And we've all got to heal. We've got to go on as normal. It's important to be normal, so as not to be strange. Remember when you're a kid, and you get in trouble for fighting. You know the other kid started it. You know you're innocent. You try to explain this, but the adult never wants to know who started it. Never cares who's to blame. Everyone gets in trouble equally. So one of the first things you learn about civilization is that there's no justice. It's immature to focus on who smashed the life out of my tiny sister. The important thing is that we come together as a community and forget about it. Now me, I find this strange. And I don't think I'm the only one.

SPIRE. *(coming forward, with great animation)* Then the drums start, there's music, boom boom boom, boom boom boom, we see the waves dying upstage, there's a blue cloth, boom boom boom.

(SPIRE places BOY 2 and GIRL 3 in position miming the part of the dying sea, drifting down to the floor, then places KELLY, SASS, and BOY 3 in front. The actors make frozen masks of their faces.)

Agamemnon gives up. He realizes he can't sacrifice his daughter.

(SASS and BOY 3 execute abstract movements.)

BOY 3. Cruel is fate. The gods laugh at me.

SASS. Still waters carry no man to war.

SPIRE. Good. Let's try that again, a little cleaner. And go.

(**SASS** and **BOY 3** repeat movements.)

BOY 3. Cruel is fate. The gods laugh at me.

SASS. Still waters carry no man to war.

SPIRE. Excellent. And…

KELLY. (with a grand gesture) Wait.

(long pause)

SPIRE. Do you need your line, Kelly?

KELLY. Can I take off my mask here?

(beat)

SPIRE. No, of course not.

(beat)

KELLY. I need to take off my mask here.

(beat)

SPIRE. We're doing the play in masks.

(**KELLY** drops her pose.)

KELLY. Iphigeneia decides here to give up her life. So that her Dad can go to war. So that the gods will make the wind blow and her Dad can go to war. She decides that something is happening which is bigger than her life.

SPIRE. Yes. It's a Greek tragedy. That's why we do it in masks. Because she's an icon.

KELLY. She's also a little girl. She decides to die. It's like Hamlet or something.

SPIRE. No, it's not.

KELLY. Yes, it is.

SPIRE. (putting his arm around her) Kelly, I understand how you feel, but we have a lot of work to get through today.

KELLY. Let me try it once without the mask. Just once, so you can see.

SPIRE. (in the interest of peace) Fine.

SASS. Do you want us to do our movement again?

SPIRE. No thank you, Sass. Just go from "Wait."

(Everyone resumes position.)

KELLY. Wait.

(She mimes removing her mask.)

Let me be sacrificed. Let me become the wind. Let me die a virgin to be born a woman. When will this chance come again? Let me go singing, Father. Let the virgins of Aulis hear me, and for a thousand years let them sing the sad song of Iphigeneia, who gave her life for the glory of her father, for the glory of her people. Let them sing of her beauty. Of the sacrifice she made gladly, nobly, beautifully, singing, how she flew like a seabird to paradise. I ask you, Father, let me have this. Let me have my moment.

BOY 3. What man has been blessed with such a daughter? I bow to you, Iphigeneia.

(BOY 3 bows. BOY 2 and GIRL 3 dance a dance of the wild sea, miming tambourines.)

Look, the sea rises in fury! Prepare a funeral feast worthy of such a heroine!

(BOY 3 exits. With a cry of lamentation, SASS executes a stylized movement of rending her garments.)

SPIRE. Hold it, Sass. Let's try something simpler.

SASS. I thought I was doing it right.

SPIRE. Try – just go to her and embrace her.

(With a cry of lamentation, SASS invents a grand gesture of embracing.)

No, no. Something very small.

(He demonstrates, crossing to KELLY and embracing her. KELLY does not acknowledge him, facing front, head held high.)

Like that. Yes?

(He moves downstage to watch. **SASS** *replicates his movements. A moment of stillness.)*

BOY 6. *(at restaurant window)* Pig scramble!!!

GIRL 4. Oh for God's sake.

(Flashing lights bounce off the window as we hear police cars screeching up outside.)

THE WAITER. Back door! Through the kitchen!

BOY 1. Fifteen minutes! My house!

GIRL 1. Your *house?*

BOY 1. Yes! Go!

(As everyone scatters, **BOY 1** *hesitates, returns, opens the tall cabinet, and removes a cake. He rushes out carrying it. The restaurant is empty.)*

ACT THREE

(A suburban living room. Somewhat cramped, too much furniture for the space. Again, this set is smaller than the set for Act Two – maybe this set fits inside it.)

(The conversation area is arranged facing the audience, so there must be an [invisible] entertainment center on the fourth wall. Upstage, three steps lead down to a sunken entrance foyer with a large hanging light fixture, a chrome and glass monstrosity from the Sixties. We can see the upper part of the large front door far upstage; it is ajar. There are not enough lamps, and the room will remain somewhat dim. There is a window or skylight through which can be seen the full moon.)

(There is a hunting rifle mounted on the wall.)

(BOY 1 *sits alone, brooding. The cake sits on a sideboard, a knife, paper plates, and plastic forks laid out beside it.)*

(The front door opens and closes, remaining ajar, as **BOYS AND GIRLS** *start to appear and silently ascend the steps to the living room. They find places to sit or lean, looking tired and a bit apprehensive about their surroundings, but still solemn.* **BOY 1** *counts them silently. All but* **GIRL 1** *and* **THE WAITER** *are present. They wait.)*

(THE WAITER [SPIRE] *hurries in, closing the front door behind him. He ascends to the living room and sits opposite* **GIRL 4 [SMICK]**, *who has found a comfy chair.)*

SMICK. Welcome to my office. There's a guy sells sundae on a stick over by the bird sanctuary.

SPIRE. Sorry I'm late. The play. Endless details.

SMICK. I completely understand. Life upon the wicked stage.

SPIRE. So, as I understand, you speak for the brothers – ?

SMICK. Bellozetti. Umberto and Francesco. *Superman V, Supergirl II, The Elephant Man II, The Return of Lolita.* They've been moving into more prestigious projects.

SPIRE. This will be a serious film. People will see the reality of violence in America, not the make-believe movie violence. People will see what it is like to live in a country where you can walk into a 7-11 store and buy a gun. It's my belief that this has a psychological effect. It makes the answers to problems seem very simple. It makes killing seem very simple. What happens? It *becomes* very simple. This is the truth people do not want to hear. This film will stir up trouble.

SMICK. I understand.

SPIRE. But with very hot young actors. Who can act.

SMICK. Mr. Spire, this is the moment when I must say, I admire your ambition.

SPIRE. There must be other people making films about this murder?

SMICK. None in your class.

SPIRE. But there are some – ?

SMICK. *(dismissive)* Movies of the week. Only you can explore the underbelly. That's what drew my clients to your proposal. The idea of a hard-hitting, independent vision.

SPIRE. But big.

SMICK. We always think big. So do you. That's why, if I may inject a personal note, I am so excited about this project I can barely sit down.

SPIRE. I want to be clear. I can't cut costs on my vision.

SMICK. Don't worry. Please. Let me worry.

SPIRE. The most important thing, as I see it, is to secure the actor who will play Millicent. Now, I have an idea for this. But I must have a screen test.

SMICK. It is a pleasure to say to you my five favorite words: tell me what you need.

(**GIRL 3 [REESE]** *moves to center, adjusting her hair in a mirror.* **SPIRE** *and* **SMICK** *withdraw to the perimeter of the room.* **BOY 1 [PORTER]** *remains seated, brooding, in the conversation area.*)

REESE. Do you have a lot of homework tonight, Porter?

PORTER. Done.

REESE. What are you going to do while your father and I are out?

PORTER. Think.

REESE. What are you thinking about these days?

PORTER. Black holes.

REESE. What about black holes?

PORTER. It occurred to me this morning, while I was brushing my teeth, that they don't exist.

REESE. *(distracted by mirror)* Your teeth?

HAMILTON. *(entering the scene)* Ready?

(sees **PORTER***)*

What are you up to, sport?

PORTER. Nothing.

HAMILTON. Don't be like that.

PORTER. OK, I'm brooding.

REESE. Are you lonely?

PORTER. No.

HAMILTON. Hey, why don't you come with us? Throw on a tie.

PORTER. I don't care for Northern Italian.

HAMILTON. We'll go somewhere else.

PORTER. Thanks, I'm OK.

HAMILTON. I know that things are awkward for you, Porter. This district attorney thing is an ugly business. But I promise you, it'll be over soon. There's going to be a story on the news tomorrow about Peter Twitchell's college job volunteering at a shelter in Baltimore. Know why he was asked to leave? He was witnessed making improper attentions to the male children.

PORTER. Making attentions? Is that, in fact, English?

HAMILTON. It's sad that a man like that should feel so guilty about his own disease that he wants to destroy others. Anyway, after tomorrow he'll pull out of the race. No more campaign ads with those photoshopped mug shots of your mom and dad.

PORTER. I'm impressed you can still make things happen.

HAMILTON. Oh, I can make things happen.

(REESE *comes behind* PORTER *and puts her hands on his shoulders.*)

REESE. You're not alone, Porter. None of us are alone.

(PORTER *looks up at her.*)

PORTER. I know.

HAMILTON. Well, I offered. We'd better get going. Don't wait up.

REESE. (*kissing the top of* PORTER*'s head*) I hope you go on brushing them whether they exist or not.

(HAMILTON *and* REESE *withdraw to the perimeter of the room,* HAMILTON *turning off a couple of lamps as they go.* PORTER *sits in the near-dark for a moment, then lights a candle. In the shadows, one of the* BOYS *produces an acoustic guitar and begins to play.*)

PORTER. Can you hear them? From where you are? Is every word they speak like an icicle pushed under your fingernails?

(*In the shadows, one of the* GIRLS *begins to sing Billie Holiday's "Don't Explain."* Some of the* BOYS AND GIRLS *sitting around the room light candles as well, creating a churchlike atmosphere.*)

It's a terrible thing you ask for. I hope you know that. Everything may seem grey and indifferent where you are, but from here it's a lot to ask. All our stories have been braided into yours. We didn't notice when it

---

* Please see Music Use Note on Page 3.

happened. Was it when you died? When you left your home? When the war began? It seems obvious now that bringing you from Kosovo to this suburb was like hanging a freshly killed chicken in the Perdue Prime Parts aisle.

(He kneels in the middle of the floor, facing downstage.)

PORTER. *(cont.)* Let us pray.

(He closes his eyes. "Don't Explain" swells. The front door opens and **GIRL 1 [KELLY]** *ascends to the top of the stairs.* **PORTER** *does not move.* **KELLY** *slips her coat off her shoulders. It falls to the floor. She pulls off her sweater. She comes downstage of* **PORTER** *and kneels by him. He opens his eyes. The two of them start to undress. The song comes to an end. The* **BOYS AND GIRLS** *lean in and blow out all the candles.)*

(The **BOYS AND GIRLS** *shift position, silhouetted by the light in the foyer.* **BOY 6 [JAKE]** *switches on a lamp to illuminate* **SMICK,** *in the same chair as before.)*

SMICK. Welcome to my office. There's a guy sells amazing falafel over by the penguin tank.

*(***JAKE** *sits across from* **SMICK** *and regards him stonily.)*

He has hot dogs too.

(no response)

Hey – what do you call the ratio of the circumference of an igloo to its diameter?

(short pause)

Eskimo pi.

(long pause)

JAKE. I need three TEC DC-9 semiautomatic handguns, three .30-06 Remington rifles, three AK41's, a Ruger .44 magnum, an FIE .380, a hundred rounds of ammunition, a dozen 20-pound liquefied petroleum gas tanks, and an antique P-08 Nazi Luger.

SMICK. *(avoiding his eyes)* I can help you with that.

(The performance. **SASS** *stands on a table as* **CLYTEM-NESTRA**.*)*

SASS. That's right, Elektra! I watched your father die! I revenged my daughter Iphigeneia, the innocent girl he killed to satisfy his lust for glory. All the years he was away at war, I thought only of my revenge. I thought only of bathing in his warm blood. And the moment he returned to the house, my moment came. Unnatural crimes such as his cannot be left to lie. Now all is set right, so climb out of the dirt and take your place.

(CLYTEMNESTRA *sweeps off.)*

KELLY. *(from the dirt, quietly, as Elektra)* And I think only of his eyes, mother. His eyes which were open, fixed, the blood of his wounds running into them and staining the whites as your lover dragged him by his head from the bath and through the house,–

(spontaneously deviating from the script)

– to the basement where he was tied with duct tape.

(back on script)

I think only of my revenge. My moment. The moment when my brother will return and join my sister and I in slashing your throat, and the throat of your lover, and the throats of the hundred men who obeyed you, and the throats of the chargers you proudly rode, and the throats of the hounds that licked your sandals. I think only of the steaming blood which will fog the air, the sun which will suck it upwards, the clean chill earth which will remain, and the mad dance we three will dance.

(KELLY *remains still. Everyone stands and applauds, gathering around the cake.* **SMICK** *takes charge of slicing and serving it.)*

HAMILTON. Are you sure that was the last act? I almost feel like I should go back in there. We've been here all day.

REESE. You have to admire the set.

HENRY. Yes, it's very…red.

HAMILTON. How much do those smoke machines cost, that's what I want to know.

JINX. Do you think it's too long, Mr. Smick?

SMICK. Hey, don't ask me. The only play I've seen is *A Christmas Carol.*

HAMILTON. Where's Kelly?

REESE. She did a wonderful job.

HENRY. Thank you.

HAMILTON. What's her next starring role?

HENRY. College, I hope.

HAMILTON. It's never too soon to start thinking.

REESE. He and Porter are already arguing about it.

HAMILTON. Naturally he doesn't think American universities are up to his standards.

REESE. I couldn't bear it if he went to Europe. It's too far.

HENRY. He can always go for a year later on.

HAMILTON. That's what I tell him.

(The group breaks to reveal **PORTER** *and* **KELLY** *lying together on the floor.)*

KELLY. They sat there for almost nine hours and afterwards they didn't talk about it at all. We talked about killing. They talked about scholarships. They talked about parking. They talked about the cake. I died twice in that play. They watched me. I used to think about what it would be like if I died. Now I know what it'll be like. It'll be something that just happened. It won't matter how, or who did it. Everyone will heal. I can die. You can die.

*(***PORTER** *touches her.)*

KELLY. Wow. I want to hurt them.

PORTER. I wonder if it's possible.

(The sound of footsteps descending a stairway is heard, off. Everyone exchanges glances. **BOY 1** *gestures for calm and exits. Barely audible voices off. Beat. The footsteps go back upstairs.* **BOY 1** *returns and makes a rolling*

gesture with his index finger which might mean "continue" and might mean "hurry up.")

(**SMICK** *escorts* **KELLY** *to center, where* **SPIRE** *waits.*)

SMICK. Sorry. We ran into Christmas-shopping traffic out by the mall.

SPIRE. Christmas shopping already?

SMICK. I know.

SPIRE. Thank you for coming, Kelly. If you could stand here…

SMICK. Now remember, the camera is your friend. The camera loves you.

SPIRE. Did you look at the script?

KELLY. Yeah.

SPIRE. Let's try on page 15. Just relax, don't do a lot. The camera is very close on you.

KELLY. *(reading from script)* I don't *want* to meet Oprah again. I hate Oprah. I want to go back home. I don't want to be here.

SPIRE. Iggy, could you read…?

SMICK. *(reading from script)* I'm sorry, Millicent, but you can't go back home. Your home isn't there anymore. I know it's hard for you to understand. I'm your mommy now.

KELLY. I hate American food. It's weird.

SMICK. I want to be your mommy. Why won't you let me be your mommy?

KELLY. You're scaring me.

SMICK. Why won't you let me?

KELLY. Stop it! You're scaring me, Mommy!

SMICK. What? What did you call me?

KELLY. Mommy. Mommy.

SMICK. *(flatly)* Oh, Millicent.

SPIRE. OK, good. Do you feel OK about putting down the script and improvising with this?

KELLY. Sure.

SPIRE. I'll be Mommy. You improvise. For the camera
for me.

KELLY. OK.

SPIRE. I'm sorry, Millicent, but you can't go back home.
Home doesn't exist anymore.

KELLY. No. I remember. There's a pool of blood there. No
more house.

(pause)

SPIRE. I want to be your mommy now.

KELLY. It gets so cold in my room at night. Can I have more
blankets? I want to make a little mound. Maybe this
time they won't find me. They find me every time
and it's exhausting. Do you have any chocolate soup?
Eastern Europeans are used to a very rich diet, you
can't give us rice. We make very bad refugees. We need
to wash our hands a lot. Did you see the sculpture I
made at school? It's a little girl made of cheese. This
part wrapped around her is Christmas lights. This part
wrapped around her is phone cord. This part wrapped
around her is piano wire. I made it myself out of
my lunch and a broken paintbrush. What's going to
happen when Daddy comes home? Are we going to
push him in the oven? Do you think if I hide under
my mound I'll be safe? I can make myself very small.
I won't say a word. I know you hate it when I talk. I
promise I won't say a word.

(begins to cry)

No. I promise. I'll be as quiet as a mouse. I promise.
Please. I promise.

(in terror)

Please. Please. Please.

(KELLY *seems hysterical.* **SPIRE** *takes her firmly by the
shoulders.)*

SPIRE. Kelly? Kelly? Are you all right?

(**KELLY** *nods yes, eyes closed, trying to catch her breath.* **SPIRE** *and* **SMICK** *look at each other.* **SPIRE** *points at* **KELLY** *and mouths silently to* **SMICK,** *"She Is Good."*)

(The scene breaks. All the **BOYS AND GIRLS** *drum with the palms of their hands on a table, the wall, or the floor.* Rat-tat-tat-tat-tat-tat-tat, *seven rapid beats, in machine-gun rhythm. Then silence. Repeat machine-gun pounding. The irregular pattern of jarring drumming and long silence continues during the following.)*

(**JAKE**, *the guitar around his neck, addresses an invisible camera as the rhythm continues under.*)

JAKE. By the time you find this videotape, you'll know what I did. What you won't know is why I did it. I could tell you about the things I've seen. I could tell you what it's like to be treated like a freak. I could tell you what it's like to grow up in this town. Instead, I'm going to play a song I wrote. It's called "(Don't Touch the) Toxic Bodies in the Classroom."

(**JAKE** *withdraws upstage. The drumming continues.* **KELLY** *crawls on her hands and knees to the center of the room and hides under a table. She takes out her cell phone and punches a series of digits.*)

KELLY. *(in a whisper)* Is this the news room? Let me speak to David Shaughnassy.

(Pause. She speaks a little louder, enunciating crisply.)

Let me speak to David Shaughnassy, I'm a student inside Olympus Microsystems High School, hiding under a desk.

(Pause. Her voice shakes.)

Am I on the air? Am I on the air? They brought their guns to school. It's Millicent Scowlworthy's fault. She put a curse on us, I heard her, the night before she died. They're killing all the kids. They're shooting all the kids.

(The drumming grows louder. Desperate)

KELLY. *(cont.)* They're right outside this room. Where are you? Why don't you do something? Where's my dad? Has somebody called my dad?

(JAKE takes the rifle down from the wall and walks into the scene.)

Oh my God –

(JAKE walks up to her.)

No – No – Please –

(JAKE points the gun at the ceiling. A long, loud, final burst of drumming. KELLY screams and hurls the phone at the wall with all her strength. The phone shatters.)

(JAKE tosses the rifle to KELLY. She catches it.)

Are they all dead?

JAKE. I think they're pretty dead.

(Enter PORTER.)

PORTER. I shot Sass Tendril in the face.

KELLY. Her parents will be able to identify her. She had cat faces painted on her toenails.

PORTER. Once they find the bomb at the highway turn-off they'll push back the press and the parents a mile down the road. That'll tie them up. For twenty-four hours they'll only send in robots.

(PORTER, KELLY, JAKE exchange glances for a moment.)

KELLY. Time to go.

(beat)

GIRL 2. *(quietly)* Courtney Melinda Armberg, Robert Philip Aukincloss,

(The other BOYS AND GIRLS join in the recitation, quietly.)

BOYS AND GIRLS. Jeremy Michael Berger, Connor Paul Brown, John Andrew Calderbank, Tiffany Anne Clark, Lily Olivia Dan, Henry George Desmond, Cerise Joan Easterbrook, Isis Maria Ericsson, John Charles Ellis,

Ruth Miriam Firbach, Arnold Jacob Futterman, Martin Jefferson, Adam Christopher Jones, Julian Trent Kennedy, Timothy Krause, Andrew Arthur Lackwitz, Peter John McGreevy, Mia Alexandra Moloni, Britney Aiko Nokamura, Cooper Samuel Page, Chastity Sheila Perlbinder, Madison Ann Price, Anthony James Ruvello, David Charles Sanders, John Young Schiller, David Ingle Scott, Devon Alicia Silverfine, Connor Benjamin Singer, Erin Hope Smith, Christopher Gregory Trimmer, Jordan Mary Walker, Janet Sydney Wallace, Hunter Paul Williams, Cameron Yee.

(On "John Andrew Calderbank," **SMICK** *begins to speak, over the recitation, from his comfy chair.)*

SMICK. No further information. How can there be no further information? Good thinking, Smick. Why not procure a Nazi Luger for a sixteen year-old? They'll have no trouble tracing that. I should have said, no Luger and you've got a deal. Flight delayed, no further information. I should have driven. I should have gotten in the car and drove to Mountain City – how long would that take? – and gotten a flight from there. No one would be watching. Everyone glued to the TV. I don't have to go all the way today, I could go in stages. Mexico City first. Then Sao Paolo. I don't have to go straight to Tunis. I've got time. But the airport at Mexico City is terrible. Who's the guy who makes the passports? Never needed a Rolodex, I've got it all up here. OK. The guy who makes the passports is Ernesto – no, Juan – no, I was right the first time, Ernesto. Wait, that's the cigar guy. No, the lobster boat guy. No, it isn't. Who's the guy with the boats? Focus! Who would know where to get a passport? Sid Frith, sure, but I don't have time for that song and dance. Will you relax? This isn't the worst spot you've ever been in. You're sweating. You look nauseous. Watch the TV. Everyone's watching the TV. Check the board. No further information.

(*Silence. The* **BOYS AND GIRLS** *look at each other.* **GIRL 4 [SMICK]** *wipes her brow.*)

(**BOY 1** *begins to stack up the cake things. The other* **BOYS AND GIRLS**, *in silence, restore the room to its original state.* **GIRL 1** *returns the rifle to its place on the wall.* **BOY 1** *exits with the cake things.*)

(*The* **BOYS AND GIRLS** *prepare to leave, reclaiming their goth/Prada/etc. attitudes, waving or hugging goodbye to some, but not all, of the others, and filtering out the front door. Two* **BOYS** *share a militant-looking power handclasp.* **GIRL 1** *and* **GIRL 2** *hug.* **BOY 1** *returns with a can of soda and tosses it to* **GIRL 4**. *She pops it open and drinks. By the time she drains it and exits, leaving the can behind, only* **BOY 1** *and* **GIRL 1** *are left onstage.*)

(**GIRL 1** *indicates her eyes.* **BOY 1** *puts his hand to his face, realizes he is still wearing* **PORTER**'s *glasses, takes them off and puts them away.* **GIRL 1** *crosses her arms and shivers.* **BOY 1** *hesitates, as though he might or might not move towards her. A passing cloud covers the moon.*)

End of Play

OTHER TITLES AVAILABLE FROM SAMUEL FRENCH

APHRODISIAC

Rob Handel

Drama / 1m, 2f

Congressman Dan Ferris is being questioned about the disappearance of intern Ilona Waxman. Sound awkward? Imagine if he was your dad...

"A genuine thrill ride. As dizzying as a Nabokov-written episode of
The West Wing."
– *The New York Sun*

"Handel intelligently weaves together the threads of the story, and the characters shift voices and perspectives with little or no advanced warning... This lends much of the dialogue a witty, unpredictable texture..."
– *talkinbroadway.com*

"A cynical black comedy that's bathed in a kind of playfulness."
– *Denver Post*

SAMUELFRENCH.COM

OTHER TITLES AVAILABLE FROM SAMUEL FRENCH

THREE PLAYS

Young Jean Lee

GROUNDWORK OF THE METAPHYSIC OF MORALS

Short Play, Experimental comedy / 2m, 2f / Simple set
The Chinese arch-villain Fu Manchu, with the help of his daughter Fah Lo See, attempts to steal the mask and shield of Genghis Khan from the white couple Terrence and Sheila, which will enable Fu Manchu to bring together all the Oriental nations in order to defeat the West.

PULLMAN, WA

Short play, experiomental comedy / 3 characters, m or f / Simple set
Three ordinary, awkward characters in street clothes address audience members directly in an earnest, frequently disastrous attempt to show them how to live a better life.

THE APPEAL

Short Play, Experimental comedy / 3m, 1f / Simple Set
William Wordsworth, Samuel Taylor Coleridge, Lord Byron, and Dorothy Wordsworth get drunk, hang out, and commiserate in England and the Swiss Alps. An irreverent, historically inaccurate look at the English Romantic poets.

CPSIA information can be obtained at www.ICGtesting.com
Printed in the USA
BVOW05s0523250216

437891BV00009B/58/P